고은 시선

고은 시선

Poems by Ko Un

안선재, 이상화 옮김

Translated by Brother Anthony of Taizé, Lee Sang-Wha

POET

아시아

차례

Contents

고은
시선

Poems by Ko Un

POET

시인(詩人)의 마음

시인은 절도 살인 사기 폭력
그런 것들의 범죄 틈에 끼어서
이 세계의 한 모퉁이에서 태어난다.

시인의 말은 청계천 창신동 종삼 산동네
그런 곳의 욕지거리 쌍말의 틈에 끼어서
이 사회의 한 동안을 맡는다.

시인의 마음은 모든 악과 허위의 틈으로 스며나온
이 시대의 진실 외마디를 만든다.
그리고 그 마음은
다른 마음에 맞아 죽는다.

시인의 마음은 이윽고 불운이다.

A Poet's Heart

A poet is born in a corner of this world,
between the chinks of crimes
such as larceny, murder, fraud, and violence.

A poet's words arise between the chinks
of abusive, vulgar oaths in the lowest slums,
and live for a while in society.

The poet's heart shapes a brief outcry of truth from
his age
that comes leaking out from the chinks of evil and
falsehood.
Then that heart
gets beaten to death by other hearts.

A poet's heart is ultimately unfortunate.

천은사운

그이들끼리
살데.

골짜구니 아래도 그 우에도
그이들의 얼얼이 떠서
바람으로 들리데.

이제 그이들은
밤 솔바람 소리.

차라리 바위 보아
비인 산허리.

가을이 오데.

바위를 골라
나앉아 우는 추녀 끝

Ode to Cheoneun Temple

They live
among themselves.

Below the valley and above it
their spirits float,
heard as wind.

Now they are
a sound of wind in pine trees at night.

Look rather at the rocks
on the empty hillside.

Autumn has come

to the weeping tinkling of a wind-bell
at the end of an angle rafter that
chose to sit on a rock.

Having gone back to the world and quite forgotten

뜰에 떨어지는 풍경 소리에

그이들끼리

살데

돌아가 한번 잊은 채

도로 가고 싶은

그이들의 얼바람 진 산허리

그이들은

살데.

그이들은

살데.

about them,

    now I long to go back

    to the hillside where the wind of their spirits drifts.

    They

    live.

    They

    live.

● When Ko Un wrote this poem in the 1950s, Cheoneunsa Temple was a
Buddhist temple for nuns only.

을파소

밤이 깊어서 길은 소리처럼 깨어 있다.

우리를 위하여 멀리까지 깨어 있다.

다친 조랑말 을파소야

서둘지 않고 가자.

우리는 무슨 일에도 함부로 후회하지 않는다.

삶이란 그다지 숭엄하지 않고

또 삶이란 그다지 비천하지 않다.

하늘에는 거미줄이 자라고

때때로 별빛이 거기에 걸리며 내려온다.

아무리 큰 소리를 가진 사람도

별을 아무리 아무리 불러올 수 없다.

우리는 흔들리는 수레에 실은

빈 그릇에 밤을 온통 담았을 뿐이다.

길은 더욱 몇 갑절로 친밀해진다.

네 부지런한 흉년의 방울 소리는

지나는 길에서 잠들 때도 있다. 을파소야

서둘지 말고 가자.

My Pony Eulpaso

The night is growing dark and the roads lie awake

like sounds.

They stay awake for us, stretching far.

My wounded pony Eulpaso,

let's not hurry.

We'll not regret anything easily.

Life is rarely sublime,

rarely humble.

In the sky, spider webs are growing,

the starlight coming down is sometimes caught in

them.

No matter how big a voice someone has,

he cannot call the stars to him.

We merely put all night

into the empty vessel on the cart.

The roads become many times more familiar.

Your diligent but poor tinkling

sometimes falls asleep on the roads we pass, Eul-

paso.

Let's not hurry.

마음이 지레 바쁘지 않으면

어둠은 차례로 비켜나서

우리가 온 뒤를 순하디 순하게 따라온다.

이제 바람 자는 풀밭길을 지나서

불 꺼진 외딴 마을과

자꾸 헛디뎌지는 넓은 배추밭 길도 지났다.

죽어가는 노인이 죽음을 서둘지 않는다.

우리도 서둘지 말고 가자.

먼동이 다 틀 때까지는 도달한다.

그렇지 않으면 끝에서 기다리다가

추운 집이 달려오리라.

서둘지 말고 가자. 조랑말 을파소야

내 가난은 언제나 네 여물 대기도 딱한 적 있으나

아무것도 받지 않으려고 이 세상에 온 너에게 미안하다.

길은 남겨둔 어둠까지도 아직 길이게 한다

왜 이렇게도 익숙한 것인지

삶도 죽음도 젊은 날의 괴로움도.

을파소야 너는 내 마음 잘도 알아서

잠든 술집 지나갈 때는

뒤를 돌아다보며 걸음을 늦추는구나.

If our hearts are not hasty beforehand,

the darkness will make way for us in due order,

and follow behind us very gently.

Now we have passed a grass strip where the wind
has died away,

a lone village with lights out,

and the road in the big cabbage-field

where we often lost our footing.

A dying old man never hurries to die.

Let us, too, not hurry.

We'll arrive by the time day breaks fully.

Otherwise, the house that is there in the cold,

waiting at the end of the road,

will come running to us.

Let's not hurry, my old pony Eulpaso!

My poverty has always made it difficult

even to provide you with fodder.

I'm sorry, even though you didn't come to this
world to receive anything.

The roads turn even the darkness left behind into
roads.

How familiar I feel with

life, death, and the torments of youth too!

My old Eulpaso, you know what I am thinking so well

그러나 지나가버리자.

밤이 깊으면 술보다 다른 것이 더 좋다.

내가 내 죽음이나 네 죽음을 생각하면

너도 또한 내 죽음을 생각해준다.

서둘지 말고 가자.

가서 네 마구간 깨끗한 데서 쉬고

다음날 없이 죽는다 한들 어떻겠느냐.

을파소야 이제 절반 대중이 넘어

네 쉰 꼬리가 한 번 령을 치는구나.

that when we pass the sleeping pub

you slacken your pace and turn back to look at me!

But let's go past.

When the night is deep

I like something else more than drinking.

When I think of my death, or yours,

you too think of mine.

Let's not hurry.

Wouldn't it be fine, too, if we went to rest in a clean
spot in your stall

and died there without any next day?

Eulpaso, we're now more than half way through,

and your withered tail is making a sudden high
movement!

문의마을에 가서

겨울 문의에 가서 보았다.

거기까지 다다른 길이

몇 갈래의 길과 가까스로 만나는 것을.

죽음은 어느 죽음만큼

이 세상의 길이 신성하기를 바란다.

마른 소리로 한 번씩 귀를 달고

길들은 저마다 추운 소백산맥 쪽으로 뻗는구나.

그러나 빈부에 젖은 삶은 길에서 돌아가

잠든 마을에 재를 날리고

문득 팔짱 끼고 서서 참으면

먼 산이 너무 가깝구나.

눈이여 죽음을 덮고 또 무엇을 덮겠느냐.

겨울 문의에 가서 보았다.

죽음이 삶을 꽉 껴안은 채

한 죽음을 무덤으로 받는 것을.

끝까지 참다 참다

When I Went to Muneui Village

I saw, when I went to Muneui Village last winter,

how the road leading there

barely meets with several other roads.

Death wants the roads in this world to be

as sacred as death.

Closing their ears whenever a sound of dry wind arises,

each road stretches toward the cold Sobaek mountain range.

But life submerged in wealth and poverty turns away from the road

and blows ashes over the sleeping villages.

As I stand with my arms crossed, patient,

the distant mountains look much too close.

Ah, snow, what else will you cover once you've covered death?

I saw, when I went to Muneui Village last winter,

how death receives one death as a tomb

while embracing life tightly.

죽음은 이 세상의 인기척을 듣고

저만큼 가서 뒤를 돌아다본다.

지난 여름의 부용꽃인 듯

준엄한 정의인 듯

모든 것은 낮아서

이 세상에 눈이 내리고

아무리 돌을 던져도 죽음에 맞지 않는다.

겨울 문의여 눈이 죽음을 덮고 나면 우리 모두 다 덮이겠느냐.

Having resisted to the end,

death finally looks back from far away

at the signs of life in this world.

Everything is so low,

like last summer's cotton roses,

like strict justice,

that it snows in this world,

and no matter how many stones we throw at death,

we never hit it.

Muneui in winter! Once snow has covered death,

will we too all be covered too?

화살

우리 모두 화살이 되어
온몸으로 가자.
허공 뚫고
온몸으로 가자.
가서는 돌아오지 말자.
박혀서 박힌 아픔과 함께 썩어서 돌아오지 말자.

우리 모두 숨 끊고 활시위를 떠나자.
몇 십 년 동안 가진 것,
몇 십 년 동안 누린 것,
몇 십 년 동안 쌓은 것,
행복이라던가
뭣이라던가
그런 것 다 넝마로 버리고
화살이 되어 온몸으로 가자.

허공이 소리친다.

Arrows

Let's all become arrows

and go, with our whole body.

Piercing the air,

let's go, with our whole body.

Once we depart, let's not turn back.

Stuck, rotten with the pain of being stuck,

let's not return.

Let's stop breathing and depart from the bowstring.

Throwing away like rags

what we've had for decades

what we've enjoyed for decades

what we've accumulated for decades,

happiness

or whatever,

let's go as arrows, with our whole body.

허공 뚫고

온몸으로 가자.

저 캄캄한 대낮 과녁이 달려온다.

이윽고 과녁이 피 뿜으며 쓰러질 때

단 한 번

우리 모두 화살로 피를 흘리자.

돌아오지 말자!

돌아오지 말자!

오 화살 정의의 병사여 영령이여!

The air is shouting!

Piercing the air let's go, with our whole body.

In that dark daylight, the target comes running.

As the target falls spouting blood at last,

let's all bleed, just once, as arrows.

Let's not return.

Let's not return.

Ah arrows, soldiers of justice, spirits of the fallen!

눈 내리는 날

눈 내린다

마을에서 개가 되고 싶다

마을 보리밭에서 개가 되고 싶다

아냐

깊은 산중

아무것도 모르고

잠든 곰이 되고 싶다

눈 내린다

눈 내린다

A Snowy Day

Snow is falling.

I want to become a village dog.

I want to become a dog in a village's barley field.

No.

I want to become a sleeping bear,

asleep and aware of nothing

deep in the mountains.

Snow is falling.

Snow is falling.

자작나무숲으로 가서

광혜원 이월마을에서 칠현산 기슭에 이르기 전에
그만 나는 영문 모를 드넓은 자작나무 분지로 접어들
었다
누군가가 가라고 내 등을 떠밀었는지 나는 뒤돌아보
았다
아무도 없다 다만 눈발에 익숙한 먼 산에 대해서
아무런 상관도 없게 자작나무숲의 벗은 몸들이
이 세상을 정직하게 한다 그렇구나 겨울 나무들만이
타락을 모른다

슬픔에는 거짓이 없다 어찌 삶으로 울지 않은 사람이
있겠느냐
오래오래 우리나라 여자야말로 울음이었다 스스로
달래어온 울음이었다
자작나무는 저희들끼리건만 찾아든 나까지 하나가 된다
누구나 다 여기 오지 못해도 여기에 온 것이나 다름없이
자작나무는 오지 못한 사람 하나하나와도 함께인 양

In a Birch Grove

Before I reached Mount Chilhyeonsan on my way
from Ewol Village in Gwanghyewon,

I happened to enter an unexpected grove of birch
trees.

I turned round to see if anyone had pushed me

but there was no one there. Only the naked birch
trees were making this world honest,

having nothing to do with the distant mountains
that are accustomed to flying snowflakes.

True, winter trees alone know nothing of depravity.

There are no deceptions in sorrow.

And how could there be anyone who hasn't once
wept in life?

Weeping has for centuries been a job for women in
our country, the way in which they have comforted
themselves.

The birch trees were clustered together but they
made me, a visitor, one of them.

Although not everyone comes here,

아름답다

　나는 나무와 나뭇가지와 깊은 하늘 속의 우듬지의 떨림을 보며
　나 자신에게도 세상에도 우쭐해서 나뭇짐 지게 무겁게 지고 싶었다
　아니 이런 추운 곳의 적막으로 태어나는 눈엽이나
　삼거리 술집의 삶은 고기처럼 순하고 싶었다
　너무나 교조적인 삶이었으므로 미풍에 대해서도 사나웠으므로

　얼마만이냐 이런 곳이야말로 우리에게 십여년 만에 강렬한 곳이다
　강렬한 이 경건! 이것은 나 한 사람에게가 아니라
　온 세상을 향해 말하는 것을 내 벅찬 가슴은 벌써 알고 있다
　사람들도 자기가 모든 낱낱 중의 하나임을 깨달을 때가 온다
　나는 어린 시절에 이미 늙어버렸다 여기 와서 나는 또 태어나야 한다

the birch trees looked lovely, as if they were together with all those who hadn't come.

Looking at the trees, their branches, and the trem-
bling tree-tops in the deep sky,

I, somehow puffed myself up with myself and with
the world,

wanted to carry a heavy bundle of firewood on my
back.

Or else I wanted to be docile

like a new bud born in tranquility in a cold place
like this

or like the boiled meat at a crossroads tavern.

For I have lived too dogmatic a life, fierce even to
the breeze.

How long ago was it? A place like this was impres-
sive for the first time in ten years.

This intense solemnity! My overflowing heart already knew

that this spoke not only to me but to the whole
world.

The time would come when people would surely
realize that they are each one part of a whole.

그래서 이제 나는 자작나무의 겨울과 함께
　　깨물어먹고 싶도록 어여쁜 사람에 들떠 남의 어린 외
동으로 자라난다

　　나는 광혜원으로 내려가는 길을 등지고 삭풍의 칠현
산 험한 길로 서슴없이 지향했다

I already grew old when I was a child. I have to be born again here.

Now, elated at the birch trees' inborn winter and the loveliness of my love,

I would grow up as someone's only child.

Turning my back on the road leading down to Gwanghyewon,

I did not hesitate to take the rugged path leading to windswept Mount Chilhyeonsan.

달

활 쏘아

핑

화살 박힌 데 네 눈

내 암흑의 아픔으로 눈떴다

● 선시집 『뭐냐』에서

Moon

The bow taut.

Twang!

The arrow strikes your eye.

By the pain of your darkness the moon rose.

● from *What?*

어떤 기쁨

지금 내가 생각하고 있는 것은
세계의 어디선가
누가 생각했던 것
울지 마라

지금 내가 생각하고 있는 것은
세계의 어디선가
누가 생각하고 있는 것
울지 마라

지금 내가 생각하고 있는 것은
세계의 어디선가
누가 막 생각하려는 것
울지 마라

얼마나 기쁜 일인가
이 세계에서

A Certain Joy

What I am thinking now
is what someone else
has already thought
somewhere in this world.
Don't cry.

What I am thinking now
is what someone else
is thinking now
somewhere in this world.
Don't cry.

What I am thinking now
is what someone else
is about to think
somewhere in this world.
Don't cry.

How joyful it is
that I am composed of so many I's

이 세계의 어디에서

나는 수많은 나로 이루어졌다

얼마나 기쁜 일인가

나는 수많은 남과 남으로 이루어졌다

울지 마라

in this world,

somewhere in this world.

How joyful it is

that I am composed of so many other others

Don't cry.

인도양

운다

이 멸망 같은 적도 인도양 복판을 벗어나며
지난 오십 년을 운다

칠천 톤 참치배 뱃머리로 운다

엉엉 울음 끝
먼 마다가스카르 수평선을 본다

어느새 시뻘건 일몰
어서어서 앞과 뒤 캄캄하거라

The Indian Ocean

I cry.

Leaving behind the equatorial midst of the Indian Ocean, so like a ruin,
I cry over my past fifty years.

I cry like the prow of a seven-thousand-ton tuna fishing boat.

After crying loudly,
I gaze at the far-off horizon of Madagascar.

Already it's crimson sunset!
Grow dark quickly, front and back.

머슴 대길이

새터 관전이네 머슴 대길이는
상머슴으로
누룩도야지 한 마리 번쩍 들어
도야지 우리에 넘겼지요
그야말로 도야지 멱 따는 소리까지도 후딱 넘겼지요
밤에 늦어도 투덜댈 줄 통 모르고
이른 아침 동네길 이슬도 털고 잘도 치워 훤히 가리마
났지요
그러나 낮보다 어둠에 더 빛나는 먹눈이었지요
머슴방 등잔불 아래
나는 대길이 아저씨한테 가갸거겨 배웠지요.
그리하여 장화홍련전을 주룩주룩 비 오듯 읽었지요
어린아이 세상에 눈떴지요
일제 36년 지나간 뒤 가갸거겨 아는 놈은 나밖에 없
었지요.

대길이 아저씨더러는

Daegil the Farmhand

Daegil, the farmhand for Gwan-jeon's family in Saeteo,

a top-notch farmhand,

used to pick up a fat hog lightly

and toss it into the pigsty,

really, the hog's squeals as well, in a wink.

Even when a meal was late, he never thought of complaining.

Early in the morning he would shake the dew off

and clean up the village road,

making it look like a parting in the hair.

His dark eyes shone more brightly by night than in daylight.

I learned how to read and write Korean Hangeul from Daegil

under the lamplight in the farmhand's room.

So I could read the Story of JangHwa and HongRyeon fluently

like rain pouring down.

A child opened his eyes to the world.

After thirty-six years of Japanese rule, I was the only kid who knew

주인도 동네 어른도 함부로 대하지 않았지요

살구꽃 핀 마을 뒷산에 올라가서

홑적삼 큰아기 따위에는 눈요기도 안하고

지게작대기 뉘어놓고 먼데 바다를 바라보았지요

나도 따라 바라보았지요

우르르르 달려가는 바다 울음소리 들었지요

찬 겨울 눈더미 가운데서도

덜렁 겨드랑이에 바람 잘도 드나들었지요

그가 말했지요

사람이 너무 호강하면 저밖에 모른단다

남하고 사는 세상인데

대길이 아저씨

그는 나에게 불빛이었지요

자다 깨어도 그대로 켜져서 밤 새우는 불빛이었지요

● 『만인보』 1권에서

how to read and write our language.

His master and the other elderly folk, too,
never mistreated Daegil.
When we climbed up to the hill behind the village
while apricots were blossoming,
he never cast glances at girls in thin summer blouses,
but rested his A-frame on the ground and gazed at
the far-away sea.
I gazed too, following him.
We listened to the weeping roar of the rushing sea.

In cold winters with snow heaped high
the wind would pass under his thinly clothed armpits.
He said:
"If a person lives in too much comfort, he thinks
only of himself.
This world is a place where we live with others."

Daegil!
He was a light for me,
a light shining all night long, even while I was asleep.

● from *Maninbo 1*

선제리 아낙네들

먹밤중 한밤중 새터 중뜸 개들이 시끌짝하게 짖어댄다

이 개 짖으니 저 개도 짖어

들 건너 갈뫼 개까지 덩달아 짖어댄다

이런 개 짖는 소리 사이로

언뜻언뜻 까 여 다 여 따위 말끝이 들린다

밤 기러기 드높게 날며

추운 땅으로 떨어뜨리는 소리하고 남이 아니다

콩밭 김치거리

아쉬울 때 마늘 한 접 이고 가서

군산 묵은 장 가서 팔고 오는 선제리 아낙네들

팔다 못해 파장떨이로 넘기고 오는 아낙네들

시오릿길 한밤중이니

십릿길 더 가야지

빈 광주리야 가볍지만

빈 배 요기도 못하고 오죽이나 가벼울까

그래도 이 고생 혼자 하는 게 아니라

못난 백성

The Women from Seonjei-ri

In pitch-black night, around midnight, the dogs
of Saeteo and Jeungtteum begin to bark boister-
ously.
When one dog barks, followed by another,
even the dogs at Galmoe across the fields
follow suit.
Between the dogs barking,
endings of words such as -kka, -yeo, -da, -yeo are
sometimes heard.
They are not unlike the sounds that the night's wild
geese
drop down to the cold ground while flying high
above,
harmonious sounds alternating among those in the
lead.
The women from Seonjei-ri are on their way home
from the old market in Gunsan,
where they take greens for kimchi from their bean-
fields
and, when they need some money, one hundred

못난 아낙네 끼리끼리 나누는 고생이라

얼마나 의좋은 한세상이더냐

그들의 말소리 익숙한지

어느새 개 짖는 소리 뜸해지고

밤은 내가 밤이다 하고 말하려는 듯 어둠이 눈을 멀뚱

거린다

● 『만인보』 1권에서

garlic bulbs on their heads.

They had to sell off what remained unsold at a great sacrifice.

It is nearly four miles from the market to their village,

so they still have three miles to go in the middle of night.

The empty baskets are light enough, naturally,

but how light their empty stomachs must be,

for they've had nothing to appease their hunger.

Still, they don't suffer alone.

They share this hard life

with all common people,

with all common women.

What a good life, where they get on well with one other!

The dogs seem to have got used to their voices,

the barking diminishes,

and the darkness blinks its eyes as if to declare, "I am the night."

● from *Maninbo 1*

순간의 꽃

내려갈 때 보았네
올라갈 때 못 본
그 꽃

● 짧은 노래 모음집 『순간의 꽃』에서

Flowers of a Moment

Going down I saw

the flower

I did not see going up.

● from *Flowers of a Moment*

어느 전기

있을 수도 있고 없을 수도 있는
한 삶의 나비로 태어났다
빛 앞에서
아주 작은 눈이 떴다
어둠 속에서
아주 얇은 날개가 돋았다
바다를 모르는
폭풍을 모르는
한 마리의 나비는
언제나 망한 나라의 잎새에 내려앉았다
이쪽에서
저쪽으로 날아갔다

불멸이 얼마나 허황한가를
처음부터 알고 있는 듯
오직 위대한 것은 낙조뿐인 들녘에서
낮은 식민지

A Biography

I was born as a butterfly with a life

which might or might not have existed.

Very small eyes opened

to the light.

In the darkness

very thin wings emerged.

Knowing nothing like the sea,

like storms,

that one butterfly

always alighted on the leaves of an overthrown na-

tion.

It flew from here

there.

It was as if somebody knew from the start

how absurd immortality is.

In the fields where sunset alone was great

day was a colonized land,

밤은 나의 조국이었다

그런 밤에 금지된 모국어가

아무도 몰래 잠든 몸 속에서 두런거렸다

해방이 왔다

모국어가 찬란했다

전쟁이 왔다

폐허에서

폐허의 주검 사이에서

피묻은 모국어가 살아남았다

그 모국어로 노래했다

나의 노래는 애도이고

나의 노래는 누구의 환생이었다

또한 나의 노래는

불멸이 아니라

소멸의 노래였다

독재와 총 앞에 섰다

나의 주술이

night was my fatherland.

In those nights my forbidden mother tongue

murmured, unnoticed by any, inside my sleeping

body.

Liberation came.

My mother tongue was splendid.

War came.

Among the ruins,

between the corpses in the ruins,

my blood-stained mother tongue survived.

I sang in that mother tongue.

My song was a mourning,

my song was someone's resurrection.

And my song was a song

of extinction,

not immortality.

I stood before dictatorship and guns.

My incantation

몇번인가 갇혔다
모순은
모순의 서사와
모순 거절의 서정을 낳았다

아직도 지난 날의 어린 나비는
지상의 한 장소에서
다른 장소의 진실들을 꿈꾼다
삶은 미완의 내면으로 떠돈다

남은 꿈 하나
먼 내일의 땅 속 나비화석은
노래화석이기를

was several times imprisoned.

Contradiction

gave birth to narratives of contradiction

and lyrics rejecting contradiction.

Still that baby butterfly of days long ago

Is dreaming at one place on Earth

of the truths of other places.

Life goes wandering on, inwardly unfinished.

One dream remains:

may the fossilized butterfly underground in some

distant future

be a fossilized song.

무제 시편 140

한심하구나
지상의 1만년 해답들 답들

거부하라
돌로
동굴로

사절하라
번개로
별빛으로

고민하라
썩은 웅덩이로
흉터들 빛나는 나체로
다음날 대답할 수 없는
질문을 쏴라

Untitled Poems 140

How pitiful,

the world's ten-thousand years of answers and re-

plies are!

Refuse them

as a stone,

as a cave.

Reject them

as lightning,

as moonlight.

Suffer them

as a stagnant puddle,

as a naked body with scars shining.

The next day, shoot out questions

that cannot be answered

태양 흑점으로

심봉사로

●『무제시편』에서

as a sunspot,

as a blind father.

● from *Untitled Poems*

내일

괴로운 날은 오직 내일만이 푸르른 명예였다.

그것이 나에게 남아있는 힘일진대

손 흔들어

저물어가는 날을 속속들이 보내야 했다

그 무엇이 참다웠던가

이것이라고

저것이라고

또 저것이라고

지난 날

수많은 밤이 쏘아 올린 별 빛 아래

사랑하는 일도 미움도

내 아버지의 나라도

오늘뿐이라면

차라리 빈 잔 그대로 두어 권하지 말라

Tomorrow

On those tough days of pain
tomorrow was my only honor, like the blue sky.
That was the sole strength I was left with,
as hopelessly I had to wave and
bid farewell to each waning day.

What was really true?
Was it this,
or that?
Or that again?

In the days past,
under the starlight countless nights shot up,
if loving, hating,
and my fatherland
were only things of today,
then leave the glass empty
without offering me any drink.

아무리 눈부신 육체와 독재가 하나일지라도

오 남루의 운명

그것이 오늘이라면

내일은 이미 저 건너 바람 속으로

한 어린아이처럼

어떤 환영인사도 없이 혼자 빛발쳐 오리라

내일! 이 얼마나 빛나는 이름이냐

Although gorgeous flesh and dictatorship are one,

oh, that wretched destiny,

if it is today's,

tomorrow will be already coming, shining,

without receiving any welcoming words,

alone, like a child,

in the wind beyond.

Tomorrow! What a dazzling name!

들국화

갈 곳이 있는 사람은

얼마나 행복한가

돌아올 곳이 있는 사람은

또 얼마나 행복한가

고개 숙여 돌아오는 길

누가 우러러 보지 않아도

하늘이야 얼마나 아스라이 드높으신지

내 조상대대의 산자락이거든

거기 불현듯 손짓 있어

어떤 이름도 붙일 수 없는 들국화

한 송이

한 송이와 더불어

얼마나 행복한가

● 『어느 기념비』에서

Wild Chrysanthemums

How happy those
who have a place to go!
How happy those
who have a place to return to!

On the way back with lowered head,
even though none look up,
how immensely high the sky is!

A sudden waving
on a hillside where generations of my ancestors have
lived;
with each of those unnamable wild chrysanthemum
flowers
how happy I am!

• From *A Cenotaph*

밤하늘 우러러

밤하늘이야말로 무언가 새로 태어나시는 곳인가
왜 이다지도 하늘에는 별들께오서 총총하시는가

페르시아

메소포타미아

이디오피아

그곳 늙은 동방박사들께서 지팡이 짚고 오시는 길인가

나도 덩달아서 그냥 잠 들 수 없거니와

●『독도』에서

Looking up at the Night Sky

Is the night sky a place where something is born anew?

Why then is the sky so dense with honorable stars?

Persia,

Mesopotamia,

Ethiopia

Are venerable Magi from those places on their way here, staff in hand?

I, too, simply cannot sleep.

● From *Dokdo Island*

아직 가지 않은 길

이제 다 왔다고 말하지 말자
천리 만리였건만
그동안 걸어 온 길보다
더 멀리
가야 할 길이 있다

행여 날 저물어
하룻밤 잠든 짐승으로 새우고 나면
더 멀리 가야 할 길이 있다

그동안의 친구였던 외로움일지라도
어찌 그것이 외로움뿐이었으랴
그것이야말로 세상이었고
아직 가지 않은 길
그것이야말로
어느 누구도 모르는 세상이리라
바람이 분다

The Road Not Yet Taken

I will not say I've arrived.

I've traveled a thousand ri, ten thousand ri,

but still there is a far longer road ahead

than that I've walked so far.

When it grows dark

and I spend the night as a sleeping beast,

there is still a road ahead on which I have far to go.

I have had loneliness as my companion,

but how could it be just loneliness?

It was truly the world,

the road not yet taken.

It will be truly

the world unknown to anyone.

The wind is rising.

햇볕

어쩔 줄 모르겠구나

침을 삼키고

불행을 삼키자

9사상 반 평짜리 북창 감방에

고귀한 손님이 오신다

과장 순시가 아니라

저녁 무렵 한동안의 햇볕

접고 접은 딱지만하게 햇볕이 오신다

환장하겠다 첫 사랑

거기에 손바닥 놓아본다

수줍은 발 벗어 발가락을 쪼인다

그러다가 엎드려

비종교적으로 마른 얼굴 대고 있으면

햇볕 조각은 덧없이 미끄러진다

쇠창살 넘어 손님은 덧없이 떠난 뒤

방안은 몇 곱으로 춥다 어둡다

육군교도소 특감은 암실이다

Sunshine

I really don't know what to do.

I swallow my spit,

and my unhappiness, too.

An honored visitor is coming

to my tiny cell with its north-facing window.

It's not the chief making his round

but a ray of sunshine, for a moment in late after-
noon,

a ray of sunshine no bigger than a little, folded, paste-
board dump.

It makes me crazy, like first love.

There I reach out the palms of my hands,

bask the toes of my bared shy feet.

Then I lie down

and expose my unreligious gaunt face to it,

but the scrap of sunshine all too soon slips away.

After the visitor has left beyond the bars,

the room grows several times colder and darker.

This special cell in a military prison is a photogra-
pher's darkroom.

햇볕 없이 히히 웃었다.

하루는 송장 넣은 관이었고

하루는 전혀 바다였다

용하도다 거기서 사람들 몇이 살아난 것이다

살아 있다는 것은 돛단배 하나 없는 바다이기도 하구
나

I laugh like an idiot there without sunlight.

One day it was a coffin holding a corpse.

One day it was altogether the sea.

Amazing! A few people have survived there.

Being alive is also a sea without a single sail in sight.

고은에
대해

What They Say
About Ko Un

POET

흔히 고은의 문학을 큰 산에 비유한다. 옳은 말이다. 시만 보아도 그러해서 가령 그의 시를 읽는 맛은 큰 산을 더듬는 것 같다는 표현보다 더 적절한 말도 드물리라. 그의 시는 높은 산봉우리인가 하면 문득 깊은 골짜기다. 가파른 벼랑이 되어 가까이 오는 것을 밀어내다가도 밋밋한 산비탈이 되어 오는 사람을 따스하게 감싸 안는다. 때로는 바위로 곧추서서 하늘을 향해 칼질을 하지만, 또 때로는 산자락에 질펀하게 누워 온갖 게으름을 피우는 재미도 놓치지 않는다.

신경림

Ko Un's writing is often compared to high mountains. It is true. Limiting ourselves to his poetry alone, the feeling we get when we read his poems is like the experience we have as we struggle along amidst high mountains. His poems are high mountain peaks, suddenly followed by deep valleys. It is certain that his work represents one of the highest peaks Korean literature has ever reached.

Shin Kyŏngrim

고은은 한국 시의 귀신 들씌운 보살이다. 넘치고, 풍부하며, 시적 창조에 사로잡혀 있다. 그는 불교적 인식론자와 열정적인 정치적 자유론자와 박물학자를 결합하는 장대한 시인이다.

앨런 긴즈버그(미국)

고은은 한국문화 전체의 중요한 대변자일 뿐만 아니라, '지구 행성 유역(流域)'의 목소리이기도 하다. 그 순결함과 그 대담한 명징성과 그 연민의 가슴 때문에 그의 시는 한국의 시만이 아니다. 그의 시는 세계에 속한다.

게리 스나이더(미국)

고은의 시들은 놀라운 시들이다. 그것들은 한국의 짧은 이야기들이다. 어떤 것들은 비문처럼 간결해서, 리 강의 아름다운 공동묘지를 상기시킨다. 한국의 그림들이다. 아니, 그보다, 글이니까, 수천 개의 인생을 시 속에 새겨서 보여주는 에크프라시스(그림을 묘사한 글)들이다.

미셸 드기(프랑스)

고은의 시에서 되풀이되는 모티브는 구름, 강, 깃발,

Ko Un is a magnificent poet, a combination of Buddhist cognoscente, passionate political libertarian, and naturalist historian.

Allen Ginsberg(USA)

Ko Un is not only a major spokesperson for all of Korean culture, but a voice for Planet Earth Watershed as well⋯ Because of their purity, their nervy clarity, and their heart of compassion, his poems are not only Korean - they belong to the world.

Gary Snyder(USA)

Ko Un's poems are wonderful poems. They are short tales of Korea, sometimes brief as epitaphs, making one think of the beautiful cemetery of Lee Rivers. They are Korean pictures, or rather, since they are written texts, they are like ekphrasis showing us, engraved within the poem, thousands and thousands of lives.

Michel Deguy(France)

바람, 그리고 하늘인데, 그런 것들은 매우 독특하고 또한 고도로 추상적인 느낌을 주는 파노라마를, 또한 우리에게 익숙하지만 독창적인 스타일, 일종의 확장된 '상징주의'를 만들어내고 있다. 여러 종류의 이런 결합은 절조 있고, 정신적이며, 철학적이고, 논쟁적이고, 문체가 있으며, 모두 한 점에 수렴된다. 고은에게 범위란 분산이 아니라 통합을 의미한다. 경험에 대한 그의 굶주린 식욕, 경험을 통합하는 신속함, 그의 리듬에 들어 있는 과민한 에너지, 이 모든 것은 한 시인을 증명하는 보증서들이다. 그 시인의 특별한 관심은 지나가는 매 순간에 거주하는 것이며 그러면서 그 모든 순간들이 끝없이 서로에게 흘러드는 것을 보는 것이다. 이 과정을 통해 그는 자신과 타인들을 함께 거주시킨다. 그것이 바로 그를 그 자신의 존재로 만들며, 또한 아주 표현이 풍부한 세계시민으로 만들고 있는 것이다.

앤드류 모션(영국)

　고은은 폭발성과 드라마와 극기적 체념을 합쳐서 엮어놓은 시인이다. 그는 말하기가 신성하다고 생각한다. 그것은 그의 무대 공연에서 아주 잘 드러난다. 무대에

The recurring motifs of his poems are generic clouds, rivers, flags, winds and skies, and over the course of this book they create a panorama that feels at once very particular and highly abstracted, and a style that is both familiar and original - a kind of amplified Symbolism. These different kinds of cohesion - principled, spiritual, philosophical, argumentative, stylistic - all converge on the same point. For Ko Un range does not mean diffusion but unity. His hungry appetite for experience, the rapidity with which he synthesises it, the nervous energy of his rhythms: all these things are the hallmarks of a poet whose particular interest is to inhabit each moment as it passes, and yet to see all moments flowing endlessly into one another. This is the process by which he inhabits himself and other people. It is what makes him his own man, and a most eloquent citizen of the world.

Andrew Motion(UK)

Ko Un is an interweaving of eruptiveness, drama

서 그의 시는 분명히 발음되지 않는 소리를 동반하며,
그는 종종 시를 생의 찬가처럼 노래한다.

《델로》(슬로베니아)

and stoic resignation. He finds speech sacred, which is very well shown in his stage performances, where he accompanies his poems with unarticulated sounds and often sings the verses like an ode to life.

《Delo》(Slovenia)

K-포엣
고은 시선

2017년 9월 30일 초판 1쇄 발행

지은이 고은 | 옮긴이 안선재, 이상화 | 펴낸이 김재범
기획위원 이영광, 안현미, 김 근
편집장 김형욱 | 편집 신아름 | 관리 강초민, 홍희표 | 디자인 나루기획
인쇄·제책 AP프린팅 | 종이 한솔PNS
펴낸곳 (주)아시아 | 출판등록 2006년 1월 27일 제406-2006-000004호
주소 경기도 파주시 회동길 445(서울 사무소: 서울특별시 동작구 서달로 161-1 3층)
전화 02.821.5055 | 팩스 02.821.5057 | 홈페이지 www.bookasia.org
ISBN 979-11-5662-317-5(set) | 979-11-5662-319-9 (04810)
값은 뒤표지에 있습니다.

K-Poet
Poems by Ko Un

Written by Ko Un | **Translated by** Brother Anthony of Taizé, Lee Sang-Wha
Published by ASIA Publishers | 445, Hoedong-gil, Paju-si, Gyeonggi-do, Korea
(Seoul Office: 161-1, Seodal-ro, Dongjak-gu, Seoul, Korea)
Homepage Address www.bookasia.org | **Tel** (822).821.5055 | **Fax** (822).821.5057
ISBN 979-11-5662-317-5(set) | 979-11-5662-319-9 (04810)
First published in Korea by ASIA Publishers 2017

This book is published with the support of the Literature Translation Institute of Korea
(LTI Korea).